W9-BLG-541

Sleep, Big BEAR, SLEEP!

by **Maureen Wright**

illustrated by
Will Hillenbrand

Marshall Cavendish Children

Marshall Cavendish Corporation, 99 White Plains Road, Tarrytown NY 10591
www.marshallcavendish.us/kids

Library of Congress Cataloging-in-Publication Data
Wright, Maureen, 1961-
Sleep, Big Bear, sleep! / by Maureen Wright ; illustrated by Will Hillenbrand.
p. cm.
Summary: As winter comes and Big Bear prepares to hibernate,
he keeps thinking he hears Old Man Winter giving him exhausting orders
that prevent him from sleeping.
ISBN 978-0-7614-5560-8
[1. Stories in rhyme. 2. Bears—Fiction. 3. Winter—Fiction. 4. Humorous stories.] I. Hillenbrand,
Will, ill. II. Title.
PZ8.3.W9363Sl 2009
[E]—dc22
2008029402

Book design by Anahid Hamparian   Editor: Margery Cuyler

Printed in Malaysia
First edition
1 3 5 6 4 2

mc Marshall Cavendish
Children

With much love and pride to my sons,
Brian, Jeff, and Mark,
and to my daughter-in-law, Becky
—M.W.

To Darwin Henderson,
who shows that the way to succeed
is never to quit
—W.H.

Old Man Winter from a storm cloud spied
his big bear friend in the countryside.
He leaned to the earth and softly sighed,
"Sleep, Big Bear, sleep."

But Big Bear didn't hear very well;
he couldn't sleep in his den in the dell.
He thought he heard as twilight fell,
"Drive a jeep, Big Bear, drive a jeep."

So Big Bear yawned as he drove around
in a jeep on a road just south of town.

But after a while he stopped in a park,
and Old Man whispered as it grew dark,
"Sleep, Big Bear, sleep."

But Big Bear didn't hear very well;
he couldn't sleep in his den in the dell.
He thought he heard as dry leaves fell,
"Sweep, Big Bear, sweep."

So Big Bear went to a house down the street and swept
each room so nice and neat.

But after a while he yawned again,
and Old Man Winter warned his friend,
"Sleep, Big Bear, sleep."

But Big Bear didn't hear very well;
he couldn't sleep in his den in the dell.
He thought he heard as shadows fell,
"Leap, Big Bear, leap."

So Big Bear found a frog he knew
and played leapfrog while the cold wind blew—
till all at once he fell to the ground.
The wind through the trees was the only sound,
and Old Man Winter said with a frown,
"Sleep, Big Bear, Sleep."

But Big Bear didn't hear very well;
he couldn't sleep in his den in the dell.
He thought he heard as darkness fell,
"Dive deep, Big Bear, dive deep."

So Big Bear padded to a clear blue lake,
finding it hard to stay awake.

He dove in deep and swam to the shore; he had never been so very tired before.

His head dropped down and he let out a snore,
and Old Man Winter said once more,
"*Sleep, Big Bear, sleep.*"

But Big Bear didn't hear very well;
he couldn't sleep in his den in the dell.
He thought he heard as snowflakes fell,
"Climb a mountain steep, Big Bear, steep."

So Big Bear trudged to the mountaintop,
where the cold wind blew and the temperature dropped.
He sat on a stump on the highest spot
and wished for a blanket and a fold-up cot.

Then he stumbled back down with his eyes half shut,
so tired he didn't know which end was up.
Old man yelled while shaking his head . . .

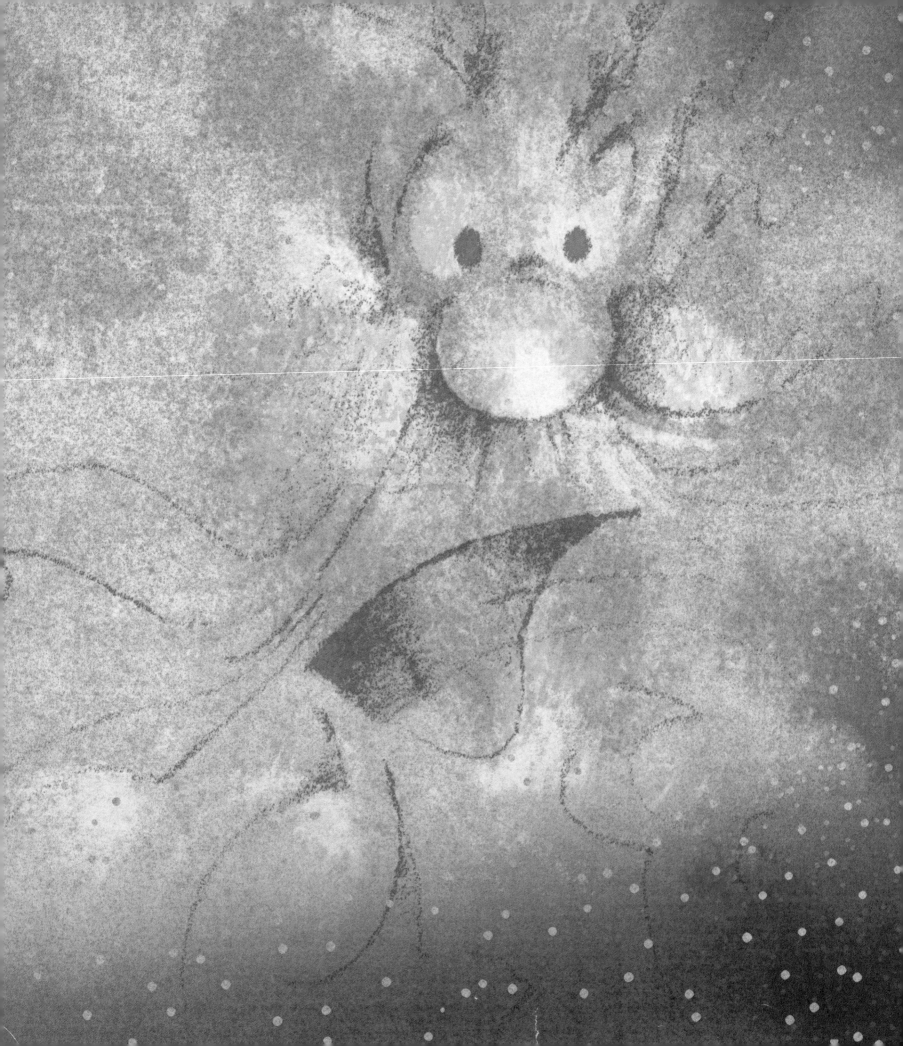

"HEY THERE, BEAR!
DID YOU HEAR WHAT I SAID?
IT'S WINTERTIME,
NOW GO TO BED!"

Big Bear's eyes were droopy and red.
"You could have told me before," he said.
He lumbered nearby to his cozy den,
rubbed his eyes and yawned again.

He put on his PJ's and blew out the light,
and fluffing his pillow, he said, *"Good night!"*

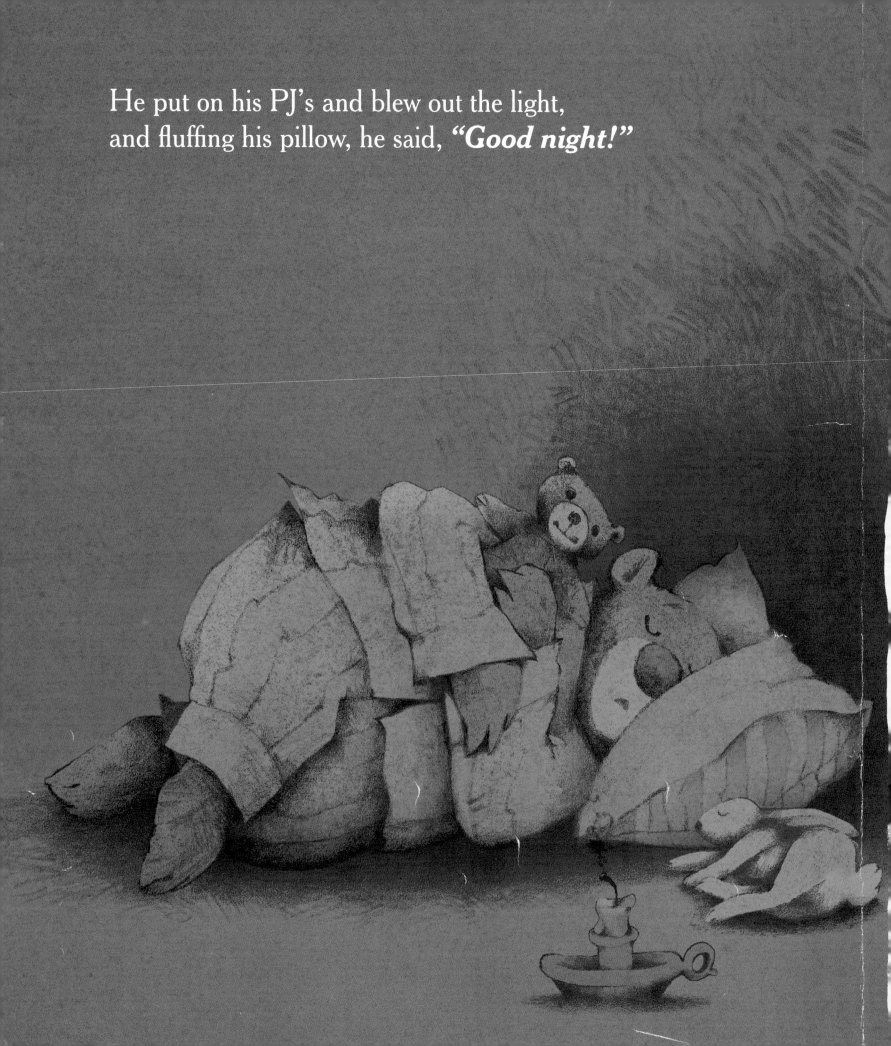